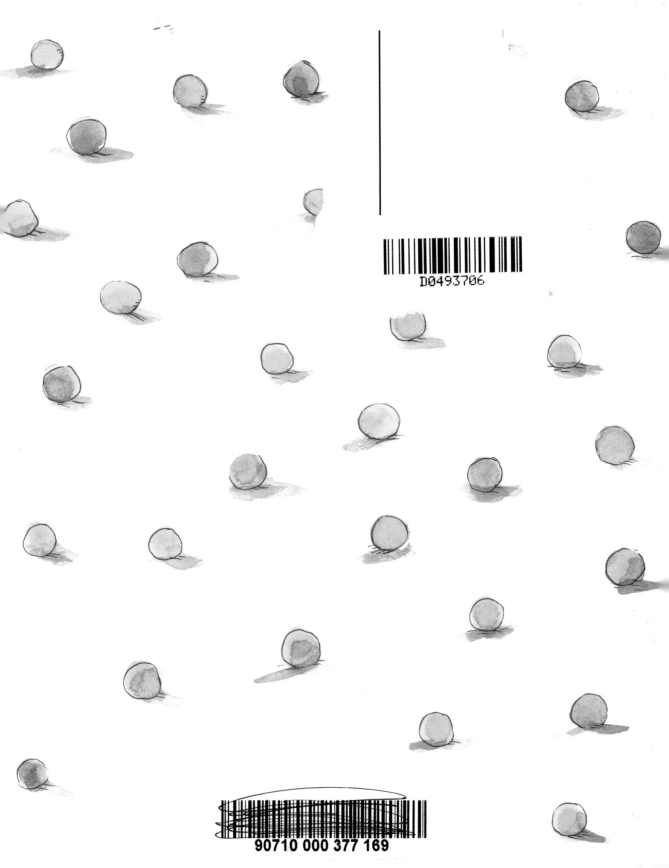

This edition first published in 2018 by Gecko Press
PO Box 9335, Wellington 6141, New Zealand
info@geckopress.com

Text and illustrations © Maria Jönsson 2017
English-language edition © Gecko Press Ltd 2018
Translation © Julia Marshall 2018
Original title: *Valdemars ärtor* © Lilla Piratförlaget AB 2017

Distributed in the United States and Canada
by Lerner Publishing Group, lernerbooks.com

Distributed in the United Kingdom
by Bounce Sales and Marketing, bouncemarketing.co.uk

Distributed in Australia by Scholastic Australia, scholastic.com.au

Distributed in New Zealand by Upstart Distribution, upstartpress.co.nz

The cost of this translation was defrayed by a subsidy
from the Swedish Arts Council, gratefully acknowledged.

Edited by Penelope Todd
Typesetting by Spencer Levine
Printed in China by Everbest Printing Co. Ltd,
an accredited ISO 14001 & FSC certified printer

ISBN hardback: 978-1-776571-95-6
ISBN paperback: 978-1-776571-96-3

For more curiously good books, visit geckopress.com

Valdemar's Peas

Maria Jönsson

GECKO PRESS

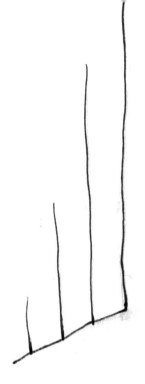

Here are Valdemar and his little sister, Lynn.

They're hungry.

Here comes Papa with their dinner.
Today it's fish fingers.

Valdemar **LOVES** fish fingers.

He eats them whole.

One!

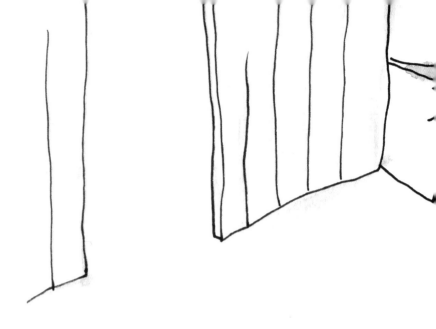

"Yum," says Valdemar and he gets down from the table.

"STOP!" his papa says. "You haven't eaten your peas."

Valdemar HATES peas.
They taste so green and round
and pointless.

"Why do I have to eat peas?"
asks Valdemar.

"Vegetables give you long fine ears.
Especially peas," says Papa.

"But I already have long fine ears," says Valdemar.

Papa decides: "The peas go in the tummy. Then ice cream. Chocolate ice cream!"

"Stupid peas. Stupid Papa.
Stupid ice cream," growls Valdemar.

And stupid little sister Lynn.
She's eaten her peas already.

Now Lynn is getting
chocolate ice cream!

"Not fair!" shouts Valdemar.
"Lynn didn't get as many peas as me.
I want my ice cream too!"

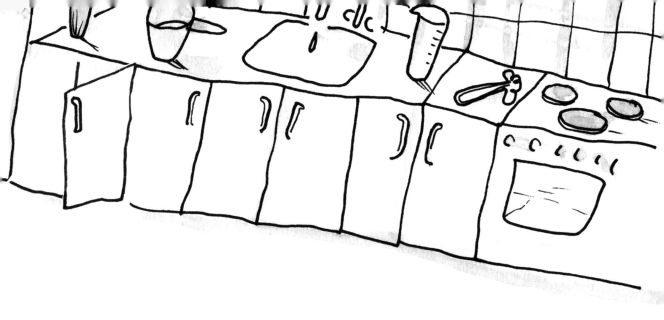

There's Lynn under the table,
licking her ice cream.

He hates that noise she makes.

Then Valdemar has an idea!

He lines up his peas.

"**Nyum-nyum!**" says Lynn.

"Look, Papa! The peas are in the tummy," says Valdemar.

"Actually, Lynn's tummy..."

"You are hopeless," Papa sighs, but he gives Valdemar his ice cream.

Valdemar **LOVES** ice cream.

Especially chocolate ice cream.

SHLURP!

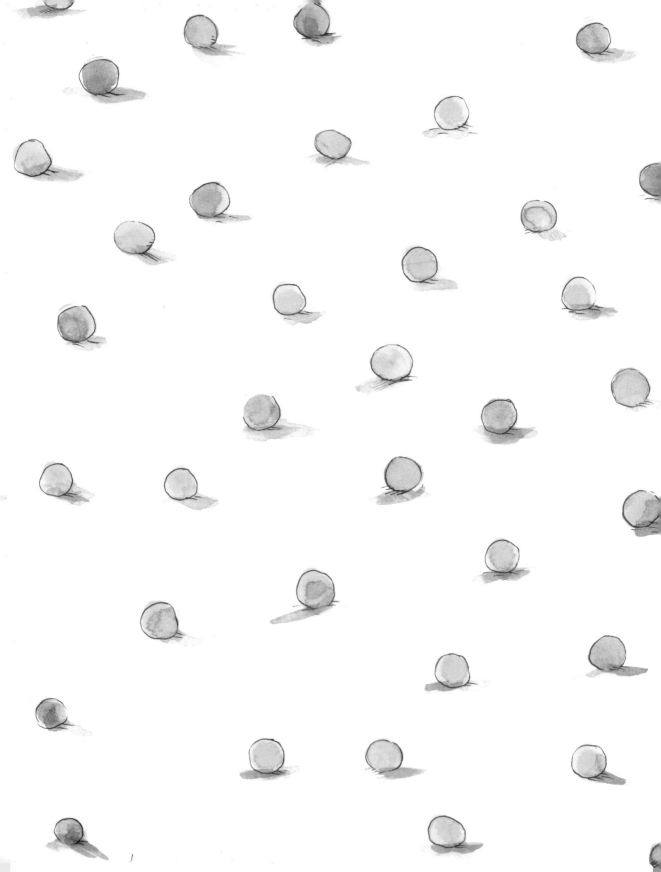